THE
SECRET CHICKEN
SOCIETY

THE
SECRET CHICKEN
SOCIETY

by **Judy Cox**

illustrated by
Amanda Haley

Holiday House / New York

J

To my students.

Thanks for all the chicken stories.

9 10 8

Library of Congress Cataloging-in-Publication Data
Cox, Judy.
The Secret Chicken Society / by Judy Cox ; illustrated by Amanda Haley. — 1st ed.
p. cm.
Summary: When Daniel's third-grade class raises baby chicks for a class project and he
takes the five chickens home for the summer, he is surprised when one of them turns out
to be a rooster.
ISBN 978-0-8234-2372-9 (hardcover)
[1. Chickens—Fiction.   2. Roosters—Fiction.   3. Family life—Fiction.]
I. Haley, Amanda, ill.   II. Title.
PZ7.C83835Se 2012
[Fic]—dc22
2011007273
ISBN 978-0-8234-2765-9 (paperback)

CONTENTS

Chapter 1

DON'T COUNT YOUR CHICKENS BEFORE THEY HATCH

"Help!" yelled Katrina. "Fuzzy escaped!"

"Not again!" said Mrs. Lopez, the third-grade teacher. She peered into Fuzzy's empty tank and shuddered. She turned to her class and held up her hand. Everyone froze. "No one move," she ordered, "until we find it."

Katrina and Sam ignored her. They scrambled up on top of their desks. "I can't stand the thought of it crawling on me," Katrina said. The other kids stayed still. No one wanted to step on Fuzzy.

Daniel, Harry, and Mrs. Lopez hunted through the room, checking the dark corners where Fuzzy liked to hide.

"Over here!" Harry called. He stood by the

bookcase. He grabbed a book. "Want me to fix it so she doesn't get out again?"

"NO!" yelled Daniel.

"I was only joking!" said Harry. He put the book down but made no move to pick Fuzzy up.

"Daniel, would you mind?" asked Mrs. Lopez. Daniel reached down, scooped up the tarantula, and put her safely back into her tank. He set a rock on top of the wire to hold it down.

Mrs. Lopez breathed a sigh of relief. Katrina and Sam climbed down from their desks. The other kids went back to work. Harry gave Daniel a high five. "That's my man," he said. "King of the wild!"

Later that day, Mrs. Lopez called her third graders up to the rug.

Daniel pushed his glasses up on his nose. He scrambled out of his seat. He slid into his spot on the rug, like a runner into first base. He liked Mrs. Lopez's meetings. She was the best teacher in the third grade, even if she was scared of spiders. With her long brown hair and blue eyes, Daniel thought she was the prettiest teacher, too.

"Our study of life cycles is almost over," said Mrs. Lopez. "So I planned a grand finale."

What could it be? Daniel wondered. The class had already studied butterflies and caterpillars. A butterfly cage hung in one corner of the room. Three painted ladies crawled up the netting. The class would release them outside on the next sunny day. A tank of tadpoles sat on the counter. Soon they'd be frogs. Mrs. Lopez really liked animals. And so did Daniel.

Mrs. Lopez waited for the buzz of excitement to die down. "I've ordered an incubator and twelve eggs." She grinned. "We're going to hatch chicks!"

Daniel shot his hand into the air. He waved wildly. He wasn't the only one with questions. Other students waved, too.

"When will the eggs come?" asked Katrina.

"How long do they take to hatch?" called Sam.

"Will we have chickens?" Allison asked.

"Can we eat them?" asked Harry. "I love fried chicken!" Max giggled. Fiona made gagging noises. Sam wrinkled his nose.

"One at a time!" Mrs. Lopez said. "Daniel. You had your hand up. What's your question?"

"What will we do with the chicks?" Daniel had a gerbil named Speedy and a pet rat named Jasper at home, as well as a parakeet named Mr. Feathers.

He also had a whole tank of guppies just waiting to be named. When he grew up, he wanted to be a vet. He sure would like to add a chick to his collection.

"Good question," said Mrs. Lopez. "We can't start this project until we have good homes for each of the chicks. Of course, we don't know how many eggs will hatch. Usually not every egg does, but we should plan for twelve chicks."

Daniel pictured twelve fluffy yellow chicks, peep-peep-peeping. He could keep them in his bedroom. He'd make them a nest in his room. They'd be company for his pets.

Mrs. Lopez clapped her hands for quiet. "It takes twenty-one days for the eggs to hatch. We'll raise the chicks for three weeks after that. So here's the deal. If you want to take a chick home at the end of our study, bring two dollars and a note from your parents."

Daniel frowned. When he brought Jasper home, Mom had put her foot down. "No more animals!" So maybe twelve chicks was pushing it. But surely she wouldn't mind one little fluffy chick? Just one?

The recess bell rang. The kids lined up to go outside. Harry punched Daniel in the arm. *"Bock-bock-bock!"* he yelled, flapping his arms. He'd tied his sweatshirt around his neck like a cape. "Look at me! I'm Super Chicken!"

Daniel pulled his hood up over his head. It looked like rain outside. "I'm going to ask my parents if I can have a chick when they hatch."

Katrina made a face. "Don't count on it. My kindergarten class tried this. But the eggs didn't hatch."

Max laughed. "Yeah, Daniel. Don't count your chickens before they hatch!"

The kids filed outside to play. Daniel was last. He didn't care what Katrina or Max said. He would get a chick.

He had two dollars left over from his birthday. But could he convince Mom to sign the note?

Chapter 2

WHICH CAME FIRST—
THE CHICKEN OR THE EGG?

As soon as the bus doors opened, Daniel jumped out. He lived in a small, normal-looking house between two bigger houses. Mom called them "mini-mansions." They towered over Daniel's home like castles.

The grass in Daniel's yard always needed mowing. It was always scattered with bikes and skateboards and toys. But the fancy houses had tidy lawns. They had carefully trimmed hedges and neat flower beds with no weeds.

Miss Clay lived in the brown house next to Daniel. She usually worked in the city, but today she was out walking her two miniature poodles, Dot and Dash. Dot was black. Dash was white. Miss

Clay followed, talking on her cell phone, her high heels clicking on the sidewalk.

Daniel waved to her. "Guess what!" he called. "We're going to hatch chicks at school, and I'm going to get one!"

The poodles slipped off their leashes. They charged at Daniel, yipping and barking. Dot jumped up to lick Daniel's face. He pushed the dog away, laughing. Dash put his paws on Daniel's legs.

"Down, boys. DOWN!" ordered Miss Clay. She trotted down the sidewalk toward them. "I'm sorry," she told Daniel, panting a little as she snapped the leashes back on the dogs. "I just can't make them behave."

"It's okay," said Daniel. "I like animals."

Mr. and Mrs. Grafalo lived on the other side of Daniel, in a big green house. Mr. Grafalo was in the front yard, pulling weeds out of his begonias. Mr. Grafalo had been a high school principal before he retired. Now he loved to garden. His roses won prizes at the state fair. Rain or shine, he was nearly always working in his yard when Daniel came home from the bus stop.

Mr. Grafalo believed in rules and order. The kids called him "Mr. Gruffalo" behind his back, because he was so grouchy. He had often pounded on the

Millers' door, demanding that they get their bikes off his lawn. Or tear down the tree house that over-looked his backyard. Or cut down their wildflow-ers, which he called weeds.

But Mrs. Grafalo had a sweet smile. She gave out king-sized candy bars on Halloween. Sometimes she baby-sat Daniel and his sisters after school. She always had homemade cookies and chocolate milk for them. Her house was full of pictures of her chil-dren, grandchildren, and great-grandchildren. They all lived far away. Daniel knew she missed them.

Mrs. Grafalo was sitting on the front porch. She waved when she saw Daniel. "Come on up," she called. "I just baked. I have a batch of gingersnaps to send home with you."

Daniel ran up the front steps and took the cookie tin. The smell made his mouth water. "Guess what, Mrs. G.?" he asked. "My class is going to hatch chicks! I'm going to get one!"

"How lovely, dear," said Mrs. Grafalo. "We always had chickens on the farm when I was a girl. I had a pet rooster named Edmund. He used to follow me around like a dog. I do hope you'll bring your chick over to meet me."

"Humph!" said Mr. Grafalo from the begonias.

He looked up, but didn't smile. His bushy eyebrows looked fierce above his gold-rimmed glasses. "Chickens! They belong in the country! Or in a stew pot," he added darkly.

"Don't mind him," whispered Mrs. G. "Enjoy the cookies. When you bring back the tin, I'll fill it again. Give my love to your family."

"Dinnertime!" called Dad.

"Okay!" yelled Daniel. He was in his room playing with his pets. He lifted Jasper, his white rat, off his shoulder and put him back into his tank. Speedy, his gerbil, rolled past in his ball. Daniel scooped him up and put him into his cage. He held out his finger to Mr. Feathers, who sat chirping on the lamp. Mr. Feathers climbed aboard, and Daniel put him into the birdcage. Then he washed his hands and went down the hall.

Daniel made his move at dinner. He knew he'd have to be cagey. Not come right out and ask.

He started while Dad dished up the tofu meat loaf. Dad liked to cook vegetarian meals. He worked at home, running a website called "Eco-Dad." Daniel thought it had something to do with recycling. Or the environment. Or both.

"Last night I saw a TV show about keeping chickens in your backyard," Daniel said. He handed a plate to Kelsey, his seven-year-old sister.

Dad nodded. Dad, like Daniel, wore glasses. They steamed up as he spooned a scoop of lima beans onto Emmy's plate. Emmy was four. She went to preschool.

"I've heard about that," Dad said. He took off his glasses. He cleaned them on his napkin. "People raise backyard chickens for the eggs."

Mom speared a slice of tofu meat loaf with her

fork. Mom was an X-ray nurse. Her job kept her busy, but she tried to be home to eat dinner with the family every night. "Chickens are messy," she said. She handed the meat loaf to Daniel.

"No, really, Mom. It's a good idea. They eat bugs that get in the vegetable garden," Daniel said. He stirred his lima beans into his mashed turnips. He did not like lima beans. Stirring them into the turnips made them easier to eat.

"Chickens are smelly," said Mom. She unfolded a napkin and tucked it under Emmy's chin.

"Sustainable food," said Dad, taking a bite of turnips. "Organic eggs. Eat local. Save money." Dad's eyes shone. Count on Dad to get excited about new ideas.

"Yum. Fried chicken," said Tyler. He talked with his mouth full. Trust Tyler. He was in middle school. He always had something snarky to say.

"No!" said Kelsey. "Chickens could be pets. If we had chickens, we could name them." Daniel smiled at her. Kelsey shared his love for animals, and for naming things.

"Me too! I want chickens, too!" yelled Emmy, waving her spoon. She hit her glass of milk. It tipped over.

Dad mopped up the spilled milk. "It's something I've considered. Fresh eggs. Manure to fertilize the garden. And chickens keep the bugs down. Without toxic pesticides."

Good! Dad was on his side. Now it was time to convince Mom. "Mrs. Lopez said our class is going to hatch chicks. She said I could bring one home if I have two dollars and a note from my parents." He looked at Mom and smiled a cheesy smile.

Mom didn't even blink. "No more animals," she said, just like she always did. "Dad and I have enough to do with our jobs and with the four of you. And what about the pets you already own?"

"I take care of them!" said Daniel. He thought about Jasper, Speedy, and Mr. Feathers. And his tank of guppies. Uh-oh. Had he remembered to feed them?

"I fed your fish," said Mom, as if she'd read his mind. "You forgot."

"That won't ever happen again," Daniel said. "Cross my heart. If you let me have a chick, I promise I'll do all the work. You won't have to do a thing."

"I want a chick, too," said Kelsey.

"Me too! Me too!" said Emmy, waving her spoon again.

"If everyone else gets one, I want one, too," said Tyler. He never liked being left out. "I'll name mine

Drumstick. Or maybe Egg Foo Yung!" He cracked himself up.

"Chickens are noisy," said Mom. "All that crowing in the early morning."

"Only the roosters crow," Daniel pointed out. "We won't have a rooster. We'll have hens."

"We could have a club. The chicken club," said Kelsey. She always wanted to start clubs.

But Tyler snorted. "Chicken club. That's a sandwich, dummy."

"Don't call your sister names," said Mom. "We live in the city," she continued. "We can't raise chickens in our backyard. Isn't it against the law or something?"

Tyler stopped chewing. "Hey. We talked about that in current events," he said. "Portland changed the city laws to allow people to raise chickens in their backyards. Lots of people are doing it. Except you can't have roosters because they wake people up." Daniel was surprised that Tyler had been paying attention in class, but he appreciated the help.

Mom didn't look convinced, but Daniel could tell she'd started to waver.

Dad took up the argument. "I think it's a great

idea. Once you taste a truly fresh egg, warm from the nest, you won't be sorry."

"Please, Mom?" said Daniel.

"Pretty please?" said Kelsey.

"Pretty please with sugar on top?" said Emmy.

Mom looked around the table. She sighed. "I know when I'm outvoted. But hear this: only one chick. Daniel will bring it home. Daniel will take care of it." She turned to Daniel. "You'll have to give it food and water every single day. And clean up all messes!"

"Thank you, Mom!"

"Don't thank me yet. It will be a lot of work." Then she smiled and Daniel knew she wasn't mad. "And one more thing," she added. "No roosters!"

Chapter 3

HERE A CHICK, THERE A CHICK, EVERYWHERE A CHICK, CHICK

Daniel jogged down the street to the bus stop. He didn't want to be late. Not today. He had two dollars in his backpack. He also had a signed note from his parents, giving their permission to bring home one chick. *If* the eggs hatched.

Mr. Grafalo was on his hands and knees, digging. His big orange cat sat on the front steps.

As much as Daniel loved animals, somehow he couldn't warm up to that cat. He looked like a giant orange fur ball. The cat's real name was Pumpkin, but Daniel called him Poison because he was so mean. Even Miss Clay's poodles were scared of him. They always hid when they saw him swagger down the street. The cat hissed at Daniel.

Daniel glared back. He'd seen that cat in his back-yard, stalking birds.

"Good morning, Mr. Grafalo!" he yelled as he ran past.

"Humph," said Mr. Grafalo. "Good for somebody. Maybe."

Once in the classroom, Daniel was first in line to hand in his permission slip. Fourteen kids lined up behind Daniel. Uh-oh. Twelve eggs. Fifteen kids. Even if all the eggs hatched, three kids wouldn't get chicks.

"How will you decide?" Daniel asked Mrs. Lopez.

Mrs. Lopez scratched her head. "We need to make it fair," she said.

"I handed my slip in first," said Daniel. "So I should get the first chick."

"I wasn't paying attention to what order the slips came in," Mrs. Lopez admitted. She pointed to the pile on her desk. "I know! We'll hold a draw-ing. I'll put the slips in a jar. When the eggs hatch, we'll count how many chicks we have. Then we'll draw that many names. Each person whose name is drawn can pick out a chick."

Mrs. Lopez stacked all the slips. She slid them

into a file folder. "Now that we have good homes arranged for each chick, I'll order the eggs. In the meantime, let's set up the incubator."

The incubator looked like a large spaceship with a clear plastic dome. Mrs. Lopez took off the top. Inside were places for twelve eggs. There was a light bulb to keep the eggs warm. She plugged it in, and showed the class how to set the thermostat.

"Our eggs need a constant temperature of about 100 degrees, give or take a few degrees," she told them. "We'll have to check the temperature every day." She put a thermometer inside.

There was a water trough, too. Mrs. Lopez filled the container with water to add moisture to the air. "The humidity has to be 58 to 60 percent for the first eighteen days," she said, putting a gauge next to the thermometer. "We'll read the gauge every day, and add water if the trough dries up. On day nineteen, we'll increase the humidity to 65 percent. That will keep the eggs moist so they'll hatch."

In a few days the eggs came. Daniel expected the eggs to be white, like the ones Mom bought at the store. But these eggs were all different. Some were white, but there were brown, green, and blue eggs, too. Some were the size of store eggs, but there were a few smaller ones.

"I ordered mixed breeds," said Mrs. Lopez. "So we don't know what the chicks will look like. They are from different breeds of chickens." She pointed to a poster on the wall. Some chickens had stripes. Some had spots. Some had feathery topknots. Some had feathery legs. "It will be a surprise. I thought that would be more fun," she added.

Mrs. Lopez showed them how to place the eggs in the incubator with the small ends pointed slightly down. She marked an X on one side and an O on the other side of each egg. "We have to turn the eggs for the first eighteen days," she said. "The Xs and Os will remind us which side to face up."

The eggs had to be turned three times a day, even on the weekends. First all the eggs had to be turned so the X side was on top. Several hours later, they had to be turned again. This time the Os had to be on top. The small end had to point the same way all the time.

Daniel pointed to a small brown egg. "That one's mine," he said. "That will be my chick."

Mrs. Lopez laughed. "I like your enthusiasm. But remember," she warned, "not all our eggs will hatch. And sometimes even when an egg hatches, the chick dies."

Daniel barely heard her. His eyes were glued to the eggs in the incubator. His chick was forming inside one of them. He just knew it.

For the next twenty-one days, Daniel was in heaven. The class learned a lot of new vocabulary words, like *albumen, embryo,* and *membrane.* Mrs. Lopez handed out egg journals. "We'll keep track of our data every day," she told the class. "Write the date, current temperature and humidity, and any changes you observe."

On the sixteenth day, Mrs. Lopez showed them how to candle the eggs. "We can see what's going on inside as the chicks develop," she told the class. Daniel held an egg up to the flashlight. Inside, he saw the tiny beating heart of the embryo. He drew a picture in his journal.

On Saturdays, Daniel volunteered to help Mrs. Lopez turn the eggs. At first all the kids wanted to help, but by the second weekend only Daniel and Mrs. Lopez were left.

"Aren't they ever going to hatch?" Daniel asked Mrs. Lopez.

"Be patient," she said. Daniel sighed. He was tired of being patient.

After day eighteen, though, they didn't have to turn the eggs anymore. "The eggs need to rest for the last days," Mrs. Lopez told them. The class still continued with their notes in the egg journals.

Daniel hovered over the incubator every chance he got, so he was the first one to see the eggs hatch. On the twenty-first day after the class got the eggs, Daniel was returning to his seat from the pencil sharpener. He checked the incubator for the millionth time.

Tap, tap. Daniel peered through the window. *Could that sound be coming from inside?*

Tap. Tap. Tap. The noise was so soft that it might have been Max tapping his pencil on his desk. It might have been Katrina tapping her toe. It might have been Mrs. Lopez tapping her ruler.

But it wasn't. Daniel looked close. He saw a tiny hole in one of the eggs.

"It's hatching!" he cried.

All the kids gathered around, pushing to get a better look. Mrs. Lopez told the tall kids like Max and Katrina to kneel in front of the table. She let the shorter kids like Allison, Sam, and Harry stand behind them. But Daniel kept his place right in the front.

The egg rocked back and forth. Cracks appeared in the shell. *Peep! Peep!*

"Look!" yelled Sam. "A chick! I can see it coming out!" The shell split. Daniel could see wet, yellow feathers. But the chick still didn't come out.

"I think it's stuck," said Allison. She frowned. "Can I pull the shell off?"

"No," said Daniel. He shook his head, but he didn't look up. He didn't want to miss a thing. "You can't help."

"That's right," said Mrs. Lopez. "Rule number one. No touching the eggs while they are hatching. The chick has to be strong enough to break out on its own."

Daniel leaned closer, folding his arms on the table. "You can do it, little guy," he said softly. "Come on, chicky."

Finally Daniel saw the rubbery membrane break. The egg rocked harder. The shell split apart. Out popped the wet chick.

"Ick!" said Katrina. "It's all slimy!"

"That's normal," said Mrs. Lopez. "Soon it will dry and look fluffy."

The chick had a big head and little wings. It tried to stand, but fell a few times before it could. Its feet were huge and it had dark eyes. Was that the egg tooth on the top of the beak? Daniel knew that chicks have a sharp point on the top of the beak for pecking a hole in the eggshell. A few days later that tiny tooth would fall off.

After the first chick hatched, other eggs began to pip. Other chicks started hatching. The kids leaned close. Everyone had something to say. Everyone talked at once.

"I think they're ugly!" said Katrina.

"No they aren't," said Max. "They look like baby dinosaurs!"

"This is amazing!" said Fiona.

"Here comes a wing!" shouted Harry.

"He's coming out," said Allison. "Oh my gosh, this is so cool."

"Let me see!" ordered Sam.

"Wow! See how it pushes? Mrs. Lopez, can I hold him?"

"Can I?"

"Can I?"

Mrs. Lopez laughed. "We can't hold the chicks until they are dry." Carefully, she scooped each wet chick up and set it under the heat lamp. When the chicks dried, their feathers fluffed out like dandelion puffs. Daniel grinned. He liked the perfect tiny beaks, claws, and combs.

When four chicks were settled under the heat lamp, Daniel turned to Mrs. Lopez. "When will the other eggs hatch?"

"They might not," said Mrs. Lopez. She looked tired. "I think we are pretty lucky to get four chicks."

In the end, five of the eggs hatched. The next day, Mrs. Lopez moved the five chicks to the brooder. The class had built the brooder out of a cardboard box lined with straw and shavings.

There was a heat lamp to keep the chicks warm. There was a food tray and water bottle.

Each chick looked a little bit different. One chick was pale cream with black feet. It had a little topknot of fluff. One chick had brown stripes. One was black with yellow stripes. Two chicks were yellow, but one was big and one was little. Daniel thought the tiny chick looked like an Easter decoration. That chick was Daniel's favorite. It peeped steadily.

"We should call that one Peepers," said Daniel. He turned to Mrs. Lopez. "Which are girls and which are boys? Because my mom said I can't bring home a rooster."

Mrs. Lopez shook her head. "This is the first time I've hatched eggs," she said. "I'm no expert. You'll just have to wait and see."

Chapter 4
PEEPERS

Daniel thought the next three weeks were the best three weeks of the whole school year. Every day, he fed and watered the chicks. The other kids helped, although some lost interest. Not Daniel. Every spare minute of the school day found him glued to the brooder.

The chicks were wobbly at first. Sometimes they fell asleep standing up. They sat down suddenly. But now all the chicks were steady on their feet. Each chick had a tiny ridge on its head where the comb would be. Their wing feathers had started to grow. A constant *peep-peep-peep* came from the brooder.

"It's enough to drive one nuts," said Mrs. Lopez. But Daniel liked it.

"They stink," said Allison. But Daniel didn't mind. As the chicks got bigger, the brooder had to be cleaned out more often.

Daniel really liked the one he named Peepers. When Daniel came to feed them, she was always first in line. She cocked her head at Daniel. She looked at him first with one bright, shiny black eye, then the other. Daniel picked her up. He stroked the fluff on her head with one finger. She closed her eyes. He could almost feel her purr like a kitten.

Two weeks after the chicks hatched, Dad announced that it was the perfect Saturday to start the garden. "Organic veggies," he said, pulling on a pair of gloves. "Zucchini! Peas! Tomatoes!"

"Beans!" said Mom, waving a trowel.

"But no lima beans," said Kelsey. "Can we grow pumpkins for jack-o'-lanterns?"

"Strawberries for me?" asked Emmy.

Dad ruffled her hair. "Strawberries for all of us. Pumpkins, too."

"But I told my friends I'd meet them at the mall!" said Tyler.

"No work, no eat," said Dad. That was that. The rain had stopped, so after Daniel fed his pets the whole family headed to the backyard.

The Millers' backyard wasn't like any other backyard in their neighborhood. Instead of a grassy lawn, they had patches of dirt. Instead of a swing set or swimming pool, they had a rickety tree house in a big maple tree. Instead of flower beds, they had weeds.

"I'm too busy to worry about the yard," Mom always said.

"Besides," added Dad, "weeds are just wildflowers. Good for the birds! Good for the bees!"

After Dad rototilled the garden plot, Daniel helped Tyler spread compost. First Tyler shoveled it into the wheelbarrow from the bin. The barrow tilted from side to side as Daniel pushed it over to the tilled dirt. Dad grabbed a pitchfork. Emmy and Kelsey poked at the compost with trowels. Mom sorted out seed packets and strawberry plants.

"How's the chick project going?" Dad asked. He pushed his glasses up on his nose.

"The drawing is next week," said Daniel. "I hope I get Peepers. She knows me. She comes when I call."

"I want a chick, too," said Emmy. "I want a green one."

"To lay green eggs. Hey! Green eggs and ham!" Kelsey laughed at her own joke.

"These are real chicks," Daniel told her. "They don't come in green."

"Didn't you say there's fifteen kids signed up? And there's only five chicks?" asked Tyler, shoveling more compost.

"So you have only a one-in-three chance to get a chick," Tyler pointed out. "Bad odds. Plus, somebody else might pick Peepers."

Just then Kelsey yelled, "Poison!" The big orange cat skulked in the weeds, stalking birds.

"That cat!" said Mom, clapping her hands to scare him away. "He's a menace to the neighborhood."

"Certainly to the neighborhood birds," agreed Dad.

Finally the day for the drawing came. Mrs. Lopez put all the slips in a jar. She shook it.

"The chicks need to be picked up by Friday," she said. "Remember, no animals are allowed on the bus. So please arrange for someone to come get them."

She shook the jar and reached inside. Daniel leaned forward. He chewed his lip. He had to get a chick. He just had to.

Mrs. Lopez drew the first name. "Sam," she called. Sam cheered.

One by one, she drew names.

"Max." Max pumped his fist in the air. "Oh, yeah! Oh, yeah!" he yelled.

"Allison." Allison clasped her hands. She shook them over her head like a prizefighter.

Only two chicks left. Daniel's heart beat so hard he thought it would slam right out of his chest.

"Katrina."

"Hooray!" Katrina's smile stretched ear to ear.

"Harry."

That was it. All five chicks were spoken for. Not one for Daniel. His shoulders slumped.

But Harry waved his hand. "Mrs. Lopez!" he

called. "I forgot to tell you. My dad changed his mind. He said I can't have a chick after all."

"I'll draw another name," said Mrs. Lopez. Her hand hovered over the jar.

Daniel clenched his hands. *Please*, he thought. *Let it be me. I'll eat all my vegetables for a month. I'll help Tyler mow the lawn. I'll wash the car. I'll never call Emmy a dummy head again.*

Everything seemed to move in slow motion. Mrs. Lopez's hand slid into the jar. She pulled out a slip of paper. She unfolded the slip of paper. She raised it to her eyes. Her mouth opened. "Daniel."

"Yes!" Daniel could feel a grin split his face. His heart settled back down. One chick was his.

After school on Friday, Daniel waited in the classroom for Dad. Today was the day he got to take his chick home. Because his was the last name drawn, he didn't get to pick. He'd have to take the last chick left. That was Mrs. Lopez's rule. He hoped it would be Peepers.

The chicks were growing up. They still had skinny pipe-cleaner legs, but they had feathers on their wings. They had lost the puffy, fluffy look. *Cheep! Cheep!* Their peeping filled the classroom.

Sam sailed in from recess. "Sorry, Mrs. Lopez.

My mom changed her mind. No chick after all. Can I have a lollipop instead?" He knew Mrs. Lopez kept lollipops in her desk for good behavior.

"No lollipops," said Mrs. Lopez, looking vexed.

When Katrina's grandmother came in to pick up Katrina, she said Katrina's parents were out of town for six months. She didn't know anything about any chicks, and she wasn't going to have any dirty birds in her clean car.

"That's okay," Katrina told Daniel. "You can have my chick. Grandma's going to buy me a puppy for my birthday."

Daniel grinned. Two chicks! That was even better than one.

Max had a problem, too. "Turns out my sister is allergic to birds," he said. "Sorry, Mrs. Lopez." He grabbed his backpack and ran out the door.

Allison made a face. "I was supposed to tell you this before," she said. "But my mom said no, too. We're moving to an apartment and can't have pets."

Mrs. Lopez looked really annoyed now. "What am I going to do with all of these chicks?" she said. Just then Daniel's dad came in, trailed by Kelsey and Emmy.

"We'll take them!" said Daniel. "We'll take them all."

"All what?" asked Dad.

"The chicks. Tell her, Dad. You said you wanted a flock of hens. Besides, if we don't take the chicks, what will happen to them?"

Mrs. Lopez looked at Dad. "Are you sure?" she asked.

Dad scratched his head. He looked in the brooder. The chicks peeped at him. They blinked their shiny eyes.

"Please, Daddy?" Emmy tugged on his hand.

"Please?" echoed Kelsey, tugging on the other hand.

"If you take them all, I'll give you the heat lamp, food tray, and water bottle, too," said Mrs. Lopez.

"Well, I guess five chicks are no more work than one chick," said Dad.

"Good!" said Mrs. Lopez. Daniel thought she sounded relieved.

Dad picked up the cardboard box with the chicks. "Our own backyard flock," he said. "How about that?" Then he shook his head. "I don't know what your mother will say."

"I'm going to call mine Primrose," said Kelsey as they all headed out to the car.

Chapter 5

WHY DID THE CHICKEN CROSS THE ROAD?

"Five!" Mom exclaimed. "I said we could take one!"

"It's a little hard to explain . . . ," Dad began.

Daniel put the box on the back porch. He lifted the cardboard flaps. The five chicks looked up at him with bright eyes.

"Just look at them," said Dad. "We couldn't leave them at school. They're so sweet." He pulled Mom over. She put her hands on her hips. She wouldn't look into the box, but the other kids crowded around.

"I'm going to call mine Daffodil," said Kelsey. She picked up a fat, creamy chick with black legs. The chick had a little tuft of feathers on her head like a topknot.

"I thought you were going to name her Primrose." Daniel reached into the box.

"That's what I meant," said Kelsey. She stroked the chick. "Primrose."

Emmy held out her hands. Daniel handed her a fluffy, pale yellow chick. "My chick's name is Twinkie," she said. "Give one to Tyler, too."

Tyler peered into the box. The black chick stared fiercely back. Tyler stroked his chick with one finger, but he didn't pick her up.

"What are you going to name her?" asked Kelsey. She still held Primrose.

"T-Rex," said Tyler. "She looks tough. Like a dinosaur. And birds are related to dinosaurs. But I don't want a chick. I'm giving mine to Emmy. She can have two."

"Goody," said Emmy. "But I'm not calling her T-Rex. That's not a girl name."

Tyler grinned at her. "No, that's the deal. T-Rex, or you can't have her."

Emmy shrugged. Better a chick called T-Rex than no chick at all. She picked her up.

Now only two chicks were left in the box. "This little one is Peepers," said Daniel. He carefully lifted the tiny chick with both hands. "She's mine."

"There's one left," Emmy pointed out.

The last chick was gray. Daniel scooped her up. He held her out to Mom.

"No," said Mom, putting up her hands to ward him off.

"But she's so cute," said Daniel.

Mom shook her head. "No and no and no."

Daniel made his eyes big and pleading. "Just hold her for a minute."

Mom sighed. "One minute." Daniel put the chick into Mom's hands. "No," she said, but Daniel could see she was melting. Mom cuddled the fuzzy chick against her cheek. "Oooh," she said. "She's so soft. I can feel her heart beating. Let's call this one Violet." So that was that.

Dad winked at Daniel. Daniel grinned back.

The chicks slept in the box on the porch for a few weeks. Daniel fed them every morning before school when he fed his other pets, and again when he got home. He brought Jasper, Speedy, and Mr. Feathers out to meet his new pets, but the animals didn't seem interested in each other.

On Saturdays he cleaned the box and gave the chicks fresh straw that Dad bought at the farm supply store. As the chicks grew bigger, Daniel had to change the straw every day. In a week, the box was too soggy and stinky to use. He got a new box, and put the old one on the compost heap.

"This isn't working out," said Mom, holding her nose. "We need a chicken coop."

"I know," said Dad. "It's on my to-do list." But something always came up to keep him busy. In between working on his website and driving the kids to soccer practice and games, he cooked meals. He did housework. He weeded the garden. He helped out in Emmy's preschool. Somehow the chicken coop never got done.

In the meantime the chicks kept growing. Their wing feathers grew longer. Their legs got long and lanky. They had real tail feathers now. They looked like half-grown hens, but they still cheeped and peeped like chicks.

By now the chicks recognized Daniel. They came when he called, peeping loudly. They liked to have their feathers stroked, and would rub against his hand. On nice afternoons Daniel, Kelsey, and Emmy took the chicks out. The chicks scratched for worms in the backyard. Every night Daniel made sure they were safe in the brooder box on the back porch.

One sunny afternoon all the kids lay on their stomachs in the grass, watching Primrose, Violet, Twinkie, Peepers, and T-Rex scratch for bugs in the dirt. "We should have a club," Kelsey said. "A chicken club."

"You mean a *sandwich*?" joked Tyler. "A chicken club *sandwich*?" But no one else laughed.

One morning Daniel came out on the porch to feed them. But the box was empty! No chicks! His breath caught in his throat. Where could they be?

He ran back inside. Emmy and Kelsey were still in their pajamas, arguing about what to eat for breakfast.

"Granola!" said Kelsey.

"Flax flakes!" said Emmy, grabbing the box.

"The chicks are gone!" shouted Daniel. "Help me find them!"

The kids ran outside, followed by Tyler, who had just awakened. "What's going on?" he asked sleepily. His hair stuck up in funny tufts all over his head.

Daniel called back over his shoulder. "The chicks are gone!"

"Someone stealed them?" said Emmy. "Bad guys?"

"Robbers!" said Kelsey.

"Chicken rustlers!" said Tyler.

Daniel didn't answer. He didn't think robbers would steal chickens. But where could they be? He padded across the dewy grass in his bare feet, scanning the yard. In the bushes he saw a familiar orange shape—Poison! And that bad cat had a chick under his paws!

Peepers!

He ran toward the cat, waving his arms and yelling. "SHOO! SCAT!" He clapped his hands hard, like Mom did. Poison released Peepers and took off. He looked over his shoulder once, as if to say, *I'll be back*. Then he squeezed through a hole under the fence into his own yard.

Daniel picked up Peepers. He held her close, stroking her feathers. They were soggy with cat spittle. Her heart fluttered under his hands. Daniel set her down and looked for the others.

A soft *peep-peep-peep* came from behind the bushes. Daniel parted the leaves gently. The other four chicks huddled against the fence. Their eyes were wide and frightened.

Quickly he checked all the chicks. "They're okay!" he told the others. "We got here just in time."

"Miller family to the rescue," said Tyler. "Daniel one. Poison zero."

Chapter 6
THE GREAT ESCAPE

In a few weeks the chicks had grown into hens. Their fluff was completely gone. They had sleek, soft feathers. Their plump bodies balanced on skinny legs. Instead of peep-peeping, they clucked softly.

Twinkie's pure white feathers shone like marshmallow cream. Violet was the tallest. She had gray feathers and a delicate pink comb. Primrose was the most unusual. Her white feathers were long and silky. Her fluffy topknot looked like a feathered hat. T-Rex still had a fierce look, belying her sweet nature. Her black-and-white feathers reminded Daniel of polka dots.

Peepers was the littlest, but her comb was the largest. It crowned her head. She had long, red wattles. In spite of her size, she seemed to be the ringleader. She liked to fly to the top of the hay bale and stand guard. At night she'd herd the others into the coop. Daniel was proud of her. "She's the boss," he told Kelsey.

A few days later, Daniel took Peepers over to meet Mrs. Grafalo. He chose a time when Mr. Grafalo wasn't home. He didn't like to admit it, even to himself, but Mr. Gruffalo's fierce eyebrows always scared him a little bit.

Mrs. G. was delighted to meet Peepers. She held the chicken on her lap like a cat. Peepers closed her eyes and clucked happily.

Mrs. G. and Daniel sat in rocking chairs on the front porch. Dot and Dash raced by. Their tongues hung out. Their leashes trailed behind them. Miss Clay ran after them, waving her cell phone. Her high heels went clack, clack on the sidewalk. "Come back, boys!" she cried.

"She should put away her cell phone when she's walking her dogs," said Daniel.

Peepers didn't even flinch when the dogs ran past. She fluffed her feathers and settled down in Mrs. G.'s lap.

"He's a very sweet rooster," said Mrs. G. She stroked Peepers' soft feathers.

Daniel laughed. "No, Mrs. G., Peepers is a hen."

Mrs. G. smiled. "If you say so, dear."

A week later the chickens escaped again. But this time the Miller family didn't notice.

Ding-dong. The doorbell rang. Mom was working late at the hospital. Dad had ridden his bicycle to the co-op to buy organic vegetables for dinner. Tyler was in charge, but he was in his room listening to music and didn't hear the doorbell. Daniel had been playing with Jasper. He put the rat on his shoulder and answered the door.

Mr. Grafalo stood on the doorstep. Rain streamed from his hat. His face was red. His fists were clenched. His eyebrows bristled. "Where are your parents?" he demanded. He didn't wait for an answer. "Your chickens are running wild in my garden!"

Daniel nodded. He was too startled to speak. Jasper clutched his shoulder with his tiny claws. Kelsey and Emmy stood behind him. Emmy grabbed his shirttail.

Daniel found his voice. "Sorry, Mr. Grafalo," he said. "We'll come right over and get them."

"You'd better," growled Mr. Grafalo. "Before they ruin my flowers!"

Daniel put Jasper back into his tank. Then he and his sisters followed Mr. Grafalo into his yard next door. The sky was cloudy. It had stopped pouring, but rain fell in a gentle mist. Primrose, Violet, Twinkie, and T-Rex strutted among the dripping flower bushes. They clucked softly and scratched for bugs in the mud. Peepers stood guard under a tall rosebush. Daniel looked around for Poison, but he didn't see the big cat.

Where was Mrs. Grafalo? Come to think of it, Daniel hadn't seen her in a while. Maybe she was on a trip.

"Get them out of here. They're tearing up my begonias!" snapped Mr. Grafalo.

"Don't worry," said Daniel. "We'll get them. They come when I call." He cupped his hands around his mouth. "Here, chick, chick!"

The chickens ignored him.

"I'll get Twinkie," said Emmy. Daniel tried to stop her, but she dashed into the soggy flower bed, stomping on several plants.

"Watch where you step!" yelled Mr. Grafalo.

Kelsey and Emmy chased the chickens through

the flowers. They tried to be careful, but Emmy crushed the zinnias. Kelsey mashed the begonias.

Daniel stood on the wet lawn. He called and called. Peepers cocked an eye at him, but edged away as he came closer. Daniel tiptoed closer. Peepers tiptoed away. At last Daniel was within reach.

He dived. And fell face-first in the mud.

Peepers slid out of his hands. She fluttered into the rose beds, cackling with glee.

"My prize roses!" shouted Mr. Grafalo. His face was beet red.

Finally Daniel and his sisters managed to herd the chickens to the fence. Maybe the chickens were tired. Maybe they decided the game was over. They stood as still as statues and let the kids scoop them up.

"Dratted chickens!" complained Mr. Grafalo.

"Chickens are good for gardens," Daniel said, panting. He tucked Peepers under his arm. His glasses had fogged up from the rain. But he couldn't hold Peepers and dry them, too. "My dad says chickens eat bugs. And their manure is good fertilizer. Maybe you should get some, too."

Mr. Grafalo folded his arms and glared. "Chickens are noisy and smelly. They attract rodents.

They spread disease. They lower the property values. They're a public nuisance and shouldn't be allowed in the city!"

Daniel just couldn't keep quiet any longer. "They aren't a nuisance! Besides, keeping backyard chickens is legal!"

"I know *that*," said Mr. Grafalo. "I'm on the city council. The council passed it five to one, but I voted against it! Chickens are allowed." He paused and glared at Peepers. "But not roosters."

Daniel sighed with relief. "Well, that's okay, then," he said. "Because we only have hens."

"Are you sure about that?" asked Mr. Grafalo, watching them leave with narrowed eyes. He looked just like his cat, Poison, when he glared. "Because if I hear one single crow, I'll call the police so fast it'll knock your socks off."

"Don't worry," muttered Daniel as they left. "You won't."

The kids carried the chickens home. Daniel's wet shoes made squelching sounds on the sidewalk.

"Mr. Gruffalo, the buffalo," said Emmy when they were back in their own yard.

"Shhh!" said Daniel, trying not to laugh.

Dad came home as they put the birds back

into their box. Daniel told him all about the great chicken escape. Dad scratched his head. He shoved his glasses up on his nose. He looked worried.

"First thing tomorrow, we'll build a chicken coop. With a chicken run," said Dad.

"Chicken coop?" asked Emmy.

"Henhouse," said Kelsey.

"Hen Hotel," said Daniel. He gently set Peepers in the box. "Nice."

Chapter 7

A LITTLE PROBLEM IN THE HEN HOTEL

On Saturday the weather cleared up. Daniel and Tyler helped Dad build the chicken coop. They used wire fencing and recycled lumber from the salvage yard. Although the hens were still too young to lay eggs, the coop had nesting boxes all ready. A ramp from the chicken run led up to the coop.

The hens seemed to like their new home. Every day, Daniel scooped a handful of oyster shell into a bucket. He knew the hens needed it to help them digest their food. He added a handful of chicken pellets. He tossed in a handful of grain and leftover table scraps. He poured it into the food tray. "Here, chick! Chick, chick, chick!" he called. The hens came running.

On Sunday morning a week later, the family

gathered around the table for breakfast. Dad always made buttermilk pancakes on Sunday. The smell of cooking pancakes filled the house.

Suddenly the phone rang. Mom answered. She talked for a while, and then hung up. "That was Miss Clay," she said. She looked sad. "She wanted us to know that Mrs. Grafalo fell down the stairs last week. She broke her hip. Mr. Grafalo took her to Willowdale Care Center."

"Isn't that a place for old people?" asked Kelsey.

Dad smiled. "Well, Mrs. Grafalo isn't young."

"It must have been hard for Mrs. G. to leave her home," said Mom.

"I'll bet Mr. Grafalo is sad and worried," said Dad.

"And lonesome," added Mom. "Moving a loved one into a nursing home isn't an easy decision." She reached out and took Dad's hand, and he smiled.

"Let's go visit," he said. "We can take her some of our fresh strawberries."

After they ate, did the dishes, and fed the animals, everyone piled into the car. Kelsey brought some oatmeal raisin cookies she'd made with Dad's help. Emmy picked a bouquet of white daisies from the wildflower patch. Even Tyler brought his baseball card collection to show Mrs. Grafalo.

"Wait a minute," said Daniel. "I know what will really cheer her up."

He opened the chicken run. The hens scratched for bugs. Daniel scooped up Peepers. He tucked her under his arm.

"Daniel!" said Mom. "You can't take a chicken to a nursing home!"

"Why not?" said Dad. "People take dogs. Therapy dogs. It's good for the patients. Why not a therapy chicken?"

Mom made a face, but she let Daniel bring Peepers.

Mrs. Grafalo sat in a wheelchair in the big room at Willowdale Care Center. She looked thinner than Daniel remembered. Soft music played. The room smelled like boiled cabbage and cleaning stuff. Mrs. G.'s face lit up when she saw them.

Mrs. G. liked the strawberries. "So ripe!" she said. She ate one of Kelsey's cookies. "Delicious!" She sniffed Emmy's slightly wilted bouquet. "I miss my garden." She admired Tyler's baseball cards.

But the hit of the day was Peepers. Daniel put her in Mrs. G.'s lap. She nestled right down. *Bock! Bock!* she clucked softly. All the residents came over to see her.

When their visit was over, Ms. Benton, the director, walked the Millers to the door. "Thank you for bringing Peepers," she said. "Our residents love animals. Many of them grew up on farms. We built this place in the country so they can have a vegetable garden and bird feeders." She pointed to the yard. A miniature barn sat empty. "Someday we hope to have animals. A pet goat or maybe a lamb." Ms. Benton waved good-bye as they climbed into the car. "Please come again!" she called. "And bring Peepers!"

The next Friday was the last day of school. Daniel said good-bye to Mrs. Lopez. "Have a great summer with your chickens!" she said. She gave him his report card and a hug.

Daniel grinned. "I will! I will!"

Daniel's backpack bounced on his back as he raced home from the bus stop. He paused at the Grafalos' house. He missed Mrs. G.

Dot and Dash raced up the sidewalk looking for trouble. Their leashes dragged behind them as usual. Miss Clay was in hot pursuit. "Come back, boys!" she yelled, waving her arms. The poodles didn't even look back.

That afternoon Kelsey and Daniel sat in the

tree house, making plans. Emmy was too young to climb up to the tree house. She sprawled on the grass underneath. Every now and then she flung a twig up. But she was too little to hit anything.

They watched the hens. With Mom's permission, Daniel left the gate open so the chickens could forage in the yard.

"Keep an eye on them," said Mom. "Don't let them get into Mr. Grafalo's garden again."

Now they lay on their stomachs in the tree house. Looking over the edge, they watched the flock below.

"Summer vacation. Boy oh boy," said Kelsey dreamily. "I'm going to teach Primrose to do tricks. We could have a traveling circus. A chicken circus."

"I'm going to start an egg business," said Daniel. He sucked on a piece of sweet grass. "Let's see. We have five hens, and if each hen lays one egg a day . . . seven days in a week . . . one egg per chicken . . ." He wrote on his palm with a twig. "That's thirty-five eggs a week! I'll be rich!"

"I'm going to fix up my old red wagon and give Twinkie and T-Rex rides," said Emmy.

"Hey," said Kelsey. "Maybe we can teach the chickens to pull it. Maybe we could build a pond!

And a diving board! We can teach them to do a high dive. People would pay lots of money to see that, I'll bet. And we could start a chicken club."

"We could join 4-H and enter the chickens in the county fair. I'll bet they'd win lots of blue ribbons. There can't be any prettier chickens than ours." Daniel gazed at the flock proudly.

Primrose strutted through the backyard. Her white topknot quivered with every step. She stopped to scratch the dirt, kicking her foot out behind her. With a pleased cluck, she hunted for slugs.

Violet, the big gray hen, spotted a grasshopper. She cocked her head. First she peered with one eye, then with the other. The grasshopper hopped. Violet squawked. Daniel chuckled.

Twinkie and T-Rex stood at the water dish. Twinkie dipped her beak into the water. She put her head back to let it trickle down her throat. Then T-Rex dipped her beak. Up and down they went, like the old-fashioned drinking-bird toy Mrs. Grafalo kept on her windowsill.

Daniel thought Peepers was the prettiest. Even though she was the smallest chicken, her red comb was the biggest. Her long, curly tail feathers shone.

As Daniel admired her, Peepers flew up to the

roof of the chicken coop. She perched. She flapped her wings. She stretched her neck. *Er-Er-Er!* she croaked.

"What's she doing?" asked Emmy, sitting up.

Er-Er-Er-Er!

"She's trying to crow!" said Kelsey, laughing. "Look, Daniel. She thinks she's a rooster."

But Daniel stared at his pet. A horrible fear formed in his mind. His heart dived into his shoes. He slapped his forehead. "How could I have been so stupid?" he said. "How could I have been so blind?" He turned to Kelsey. "Some vet I'll make. I can't even tell a rooster from a hen!"

Kelsey looked blank. "What do you mean?"

He pointed to Peepers. She looked pleased with herself. "Peepers. She isn't a hen. She—I mean *he*— is a rooster. We should have known. That's why she—I mean *he*—has a bigger comb. That's why she—I mean *he*—bosses all the other chickens. That's why she—I mean *he*—is starting to crow. Peepers is a rooster!"

Peepers cocked his head at them, as if to say *I've got it now, fellows!* He stretched out his neck again. And crowed and crowed and crowed.

Chapter 8
PINKIE PROMISE

"This is terrible!" said Daniel as he watched Peepers crow.

"Why?" asked Kelsey. "Now we can have baby chicks."

"Roosters are illegal. If Mr. Gruffalo finds out, he'll call the police."

"Will they lock Peepers in jail?" asked Emmy. Her eyes were big.

"Worse," said Daniel. "We've got to save him. Protect him!"

"I know! We can disguise him!" said Kelsey.

"Put a pink bow on him. Then everyone will think he's a girl chicken," said Emmy.

"We need a chicken club." Kelsey sat up. The

hens scratched for worms in the dirt. Peepers stood on top of the henhouse. Alert and tall. Watching for danger.

"A club? You and your old clubs." Daniel put his arms around his knees and laid his head against them. "We've got real problems. Big problems. If the neighbors complain, the police will take Peepers away. What could a club do?"

"Keep Peepers a secret," said Kelsey. "A secret club. For keeping secrets."

"I want to be in the club, too," said Emmy. Daniel stood up so suddenly the tree house rocked. "Wait a minute. That might work." He chewed his lip in thought. "But not a secret *club*! A secret *society*! The Secret Chicken Society."

"With passwords and secret handshakes and maybe a secret code," said Kelsey, pleased.

Daniel nodded. The Secret Chicken Society. Mission: To keep Peepers a secret. So nobody would find out that he was a rooster. So nobody could take him away.

"We have to take an oath. A secret oath. A double secret oath. A blood vow!" said Daniel.

"We can't use blood anymore. Mom said," Kelsey reminded him.

"A spit promise, then."

"Eww," said Emmy. "I'm not doing blood or spit. That's gross."

"Okay, okay," said Daniel. "A pinkie swear."

"No swearing," said Kelsey. "Mom said."

Daniel sighed. It was hard to take a double secret oath without blood or spit or swearing. "Okay. A pinkie promise."

Kelsey nodded. She held out her hand and hooked pinkie fingers with Daniel. "Repeat after me," said Daniel. "I solemnly swear . . ."

"You mean *promise*," Kelsey said.

Daniel started over. "I solemnly *promise* . . ."

"Wait! Wait!" yelled Emmy from beneath the tree. "I want to be a secret chicken, too."

Daniel sighed again. He and Kelsey climbed down. Daniel and Kelsey hooked pinkies. Emmy slid her little finger on top of theirs.

"Repeat after me," Daniel began again. "I solemnly swear . . ."

"*Promise!*" said Kelsey and Emmy together.

"I solemnly *promise* . . ."

"Hey!" said Tyler. He came out the back door. His hair was rumpled. He bit into an apple. "What'cha doing? A pinkie swear?"

"Pinkie *promise!*" yelled Daniel, Kelsey, and Emmy.

Daniel and Kelsey traded glances. "We'll have to tell him. He'll find out soon enough."

Daniel gave Tyler a stern look. "Okay, but you have to promise not to tell."

"Tell what?"

So Daniel explained, with help from Kelsey. About Peepers being a rooster. About Mr. Grafalo threatening to call the police. About the Secret

Chicken Society, dedicated to keeping Peepers a secret.

Tyler shook his head when they were done. "This will never work," he said.

"Well, you don't have to be in the Secret Chicken Society if you don't want to help," said Daniel. "But you still can't tell."

Tyler hooked his pinkie with Daniel's and Kelsey's. Emmy put hers on top again. They swore (promised) to keep Peepers a secret. But how?

Chapter 9

NOBODY HERE
BUT US CHICKENS

Over the next few days, the Secret Chicken Society tried to carry out its mission: Keep the rooster a secret. Daniel kept track of their attempts in the back of his egg journal.

Attempt #1: Hide Peepers.

First, Daniel locked Peepers in the chicken coop. He put food and water inside. He hoped no one would notice Peepers wasn't outside. But after breakfast, Dad came back from watering the garden. "Don't we have five chickens?" he asked. "I only see four. Is one missing? Better find her, Daniel. We don't want them loose in Mr. Grafalo's garden again."

Luckily, Dad didn't hear Peepers' happy crow when Daniel let him out of the coop.

Attempt #2: Keep Peepers Quiet.

Daniel woke up early the next morning. *Er-Er-Er!* Pale gray light shone through his curtains. He put on his glasses and peered at his alarm clock. It was only 4:30 A.M.! He groaned.

Daniel slipped out of the house. The grass felt cool and damp under his bare feet. He opened the wire gate to the chicken run. The chickens were all asleep inside the Hen Hotel. Daniel could hear their soft clucks.

Peepers crowed again. "Shhh!" hissed Daniel. He opened the door to the coop. He just wanted to tell Peepers to be quiet. A shaft of sunlight lit up the inside of the coop.

As soon as the door opened, the henhouse exploded with noise. What a ruckus! All the hens squawked. They flapped their wings. Maybe they thought they were under attack. *Foxes! Coyotes! Wolves!* they seemed to say. *Cats! Run for your lives!* Peepers protected his hens bravely. He flew down from his roost and danced around, pecking Daniel's bare toes.

"Ouch! Stop! It's just me!" Daniel yelled. He retreated and slammed the door.

"Daniel! What on earth?" Mom stood at the back

door in her bathrobe. "What are you doing? Do you have any idea what time it is?"

"Sorry, Mom. I thought I heard something." Daniel didn't add that he'd heard his rooster crow.

Attempt #3: Stop Peepers from Crowing.

Next, Daniel tried putting a muzzle on Peepers. He'd read about that on the Internet. "It isn't really a muzzle," he told the members of the Secret Chicken Society (except for Tyler, who had baseball practice). "It's more like a harness. A rooster can't crow if he can't stretch his neck. This cloth holds his head down a little bit."

"Will it hurt?" asked Emmy.

Daniel shook his head. "I don't think so. And he can breathe and drink and eat just like usual."

Emmy and Kelsey watched Daniel struggle to get the cloth on Peepers. The rooster flapped his wings. He squawked. He didn't want to wear a muzzle. Finally Daniel gave up. "It didn't work in the video, either," he said sadly.

Attempt #4: Put Peepers in the Dark.

The next day Daniel did some more research. "I've got it!" he told Kelsey and Emmy. "Roosters crow only in daylight. So if we can keep Peepers in the dark, he won't crow."

Kelsey made a face. "We can't keep him in the dark all the time," she pointed out. "It would be cruel."

"I'll let him out at eight o'clock every morning," said Daniel. "There'll be other noises by then. Cars. Lawn mowers. Stuff like that. No one will hear him."

He explained that they would put Peepers in a box every night. Daniel would hide the box in the storage cupboard in the garage.

"There's plenty of air in there, but it's dark. So he won't crow."

At dusk Peepers and the hens headed to the coop to roost, just as they did every evening.

The Secret Chicken Society hid in the bushes to watch. Daniel parted the bushes. Kelsey leaned against him. She peered over his shoulder. Emmy lay flat on the ground. She looked out between Daniel's feet. (Tyler was at the skate park with friends.)

The hens went up the ramp to the henhouse. First came Primrose, the white silkie. Her topknot bobbed up and down. Violet waddled behind her. Next was Twinkie, the tall leghorn. She clucked softly as she went inside, as if to say good night. Last in line was T-Rex. She was a Plymouth Rock hen. Her black-and-white feathers reminded Daniel of the chickens on Dad's kitchen towels.

Peepers stood guard. He was a bantam rooster, smaller than all his hens. It was clear that he was the boss. He waited until every hen was safe inside. Then he started up the ramp.

Daniel pounced. He grabbed Peepers. Kelsey opened the box. But Peepers had other ideas. He must have sensed something was wrong. Usually he let Daniel pick him up. But tonight he squawked and flapped and pecked.

"Ow!" yelled Daniel, dropping the rooster.

"Grab him!" yelled Emmy. Kelsey reached for Peepers, but he raced away.

"Gosh," said Emmy. "He runs fast—for a chicken."

Daniel and Kelsey raced after him, but the rooster was too quick. Finally, with a pleased squawk, he flew into the tree. He perched on a high branch.

"Great," said Daniel. "What do we do now?"

"Climb the tree," said Kelsey.

Daniel sighed and started up the tree. But every time he got within reach, Peepers flew higher. Finally Daniel was on the same level as Peepers. "Come here," he whispered. "Come on. Come to Daniel. Pretty Peepers. Nice chicken."

Peepers cocked his head. He eyed Daniel

suspiciously. His red comb flopped over to one side. He edged away. Daniel stretched out his hand, but he couldn't quite reach.

It was nearly dark. Daniel could see Peepers in the twilight. He looked quite pleased with himself.

"Bedtime!" Dad called from the house. Emmy trotted inside.

"Better come down," said Kelsey. "We can try again tomorrow." She followed Emmy inside.

Down below, the house windows glowed like lanterns in the blue dusk. Daniel gave up. He climbed partway down. His shirt filled with twigs. He got one long, red scratch on his arm. He jumped the last few feet and brushed a spider web out of his hair.

Above him, Peepers stretched his neck and crowed. To Daniel's ears it sounded like the mocking cry of a warrior after beating his enemy. Daniel glared at his pet. Then he shrugged and went inside.

That night he made a final entry in his journal. *Mission: Unaccomplished.*

Chapter 10

HEN PARTY

Daniel couldn't get to sleep. First he was too hot. So he kicked off his covers. Then he was too cold. So he pulled them up. Finally he fell asleep. He dreamed there was a fire. He could hear the sirens. When he woke up, there were no sirens. Only Peepers crowing loudly from the tree.

Daniel groaned. He opened his eyes. It was barely light! He knew he should try to get his pet to shut up. But he couldn't make himself get out of bed. He jammed his pillow over his head.

The next time Daniel woke up, sunlight streamed through his curtains. He'd slept in. The doorbell rang. Daniel rubbed his eyes.

Daniel heard voices from the hall. He put on his

glasses and padded out in his pajamas to see what was going on.

Dad stood at the open door. Tyler, Emmy, and Kelsey gathered around. Kelsey looked scared. Emmy hid behind Dad, clutching her stuffed lion. Tyler was eating a banana. Mom was already at work.

Two police officers stood at the door. Both wore blue uniforms. One officer was tall and thin. The other was short and stout. *Here is my handle, here is my spout*, thought Daniel. He pushed the thought away. This was no time for nursery songs.

"What's going on?" Daniel asked. "Is something wrong?"

The stout officer looked at Dad. "We've had a complaint about a rooster. Crowing. Disturbing the peace. Do you have a rooster?"

Dad shook his head. "Five hens," he said.

The short officer nodded. "Hens aren't a problem, but roosters are illegal in the city."

Daniel swallowed. "If somebody has a rooster, what happens?"

The stout officer didn't smile. "The owner has fourteen days to get rid of it. If the rooster isn't removed, we are authorized to seize it."

"And do what?" asked Daniel. But in his heart

he knew. He knew what happened to stray dogs
and cats if no one gave them a home.

★ ★ ★

The Secret Chicken Society met in the tree house right after breakfast. "I'll bet it was Mr. Grafalo who complained," said Kelsey.

"Grumpy Mr. Gruffalo," said Emmy.

"He was always grouchy," said Daniel slowly. "But I think he's gotten worse since Mrs. G. had to go live at Willowdale."

"Maybe he misses her," said Kelsey. "I miss her."

"Me too," said Emmy. "But if you ask me, Mr. Gruffalo is still a big buffalo!"

The hens were in the yard, pecking in the weeds. Peepers had come down from the tree. He stood watch near the hens. Suddenly he fluffed out his feathers and beat the air with his wings. *Squawk! Squawk!* An orange streak shot under the fence. Poison!

"Nice," said Kelsey. "He does his job."

"Did you hear him crow this morning? I don't know how Mom and Dad missed it. For a little guy, he sure is loud." Daniel chewed his lower lip.

"What will the police do if they find out about Peepers?" asked Emmy from the foot of the tree. "Will they put him in jail?"

"Worse," said Kelsey.

"Much worse," groaned Daniel.

"What, then?" yelled Emmy impatiently.

Daniel stared at her solemnly. "They'll kill him," he said.

"Kill Peepers? No!" yelled Emmy.

"And eat him," added Kelsey.

"That's awful!" Emmy started to cry. "Poor Peepers!"

"We have to keep him from crowing!" said Daniel. "We just have to!"

All afternoon Daniel looked in books and on the Internet. He reported back to the SCS.

"Roosters will crow any time of the day," he told Kelsey and Emmy. (Tyler was at the mall.) "But they mostly crow at dawn."

Kelsey nodded. "But we tried everything. What else can we do?"

"I have an idea," said Daniel. "If we can keep the coop dark, he won't crow. But to be extra sure, we can insulate it. So sounds won't get out."

With Tyler's help, the Secret Chicken Society insulated the Hen Hotel. They used empty cardboard egg cartons to muffle sound. They used black plastic trash bags to keep out the light. Fortunately,

Mom was at work. When Dad was working on his website, he didn't notice what went on around him.

At dusk Peepers herded his hens into the chicken coop to roost. Then he followed them up the ramp and went inside. Daniel fastened the door behind them.

"They want to be in the coop at night," Daniel told his sisters. "They feel safe inside. That's why birds roost in trees. So foxes and coyotes and raccoons don't get them."

The insulation seemed to work. If Peepers crowed at dawn, no one in the house could hear it. Daniel didn't think the neighbors could, either.

After breakfast Daniel fed and watered all his pets and let the hens out to forage. They seemed happy with their newly redecorated quarters. At any rate, they didn't complain.

"Everything's under control," Daniel told Kelsey and Emmy at the next SCS meeting a few days later. "We've got it licked."

But his conscience prickled. Mom and Dad were still in the dark (so to speak) about Peepers being a rooster. Mom and Dad trusted the hens to Daniel's care. Even though he hadn't told a lie, it didn't feel right to keep a secret from them.

Chapter 11

JAILBIRD

One day about two weeks later the weather turned hot. Daniel checked his pets. Jasper drank noisily from his bottle. Speedy panted in his cage. Mr. Feathers fluffed out his feathers and closed his eyes. The guppies were the only ones staying cool. They swam comfortably around in their tank, looking happy.

The SCS members sat in the tree house—at least Daniel and Kelsey did. Emmy sat on the grass. Tyler was at a ball game. Not a breeze stirred the leaves on the trees. Bees buzzed in the garden. The chickens rested in the shade, not making much noise.

"It's too hot to do anything," said Kelsey, fanning herself.

"Too hot to think," said Daniel. He rubbed the sweat off his forehead with his arm.

"Too hot to pink," said Emmy. She peeled the petals off a daisy and flung them into the air.

"Too hot to stink," said Daniel, and they all laughed.

"Can we have ice pops?" Emmy called to Dad. He was working on his laptop on the back porch. He nodded.

"Bring me an orange one," he said.

"Can we run through the sprinkler?" asked Kelsey.

"Sure," said Dad. "But set it up in the front yard. That grass could use some water."

They went out the side gate to the front yard, dragging the hose and sprinkler. Daniel didn't see the curious hens follow them out front.

The kids put on their swimming suits and ran through the spray. The cold water felt delightful. When they were completely soaked, Emmy brought out the ice pops. They sat on the hot cement steps, watching the sprinkler make rainbows in the sky. Daniel had raspberry, his favorite. He licked it. The drips ran down his arm.

"Look, blood," he told Emmy.

"Eww," she said. She had a blue ice pop. Her lips and tongue were blue.

Just then Dot and Dash ran over from next door, yapping. Dash jumped up on Emmy. He licked her face. He knocked the ice pop out of her hand.

"My ice pop!" cried Emmy. "Bad doggies!" The ice pop lay melting on the sidewalk. The poodles lapped it up.

"Dot!" called Miss Clay. "Dash!" She stood on her front porch and clapped her hands. The poodles paid no attention to her. They spotted the hens. *Yap! Yap!* they barked.

Daniel wasn't sure what happened next. Suddenly there was a flurry of feathers. Peepers! He spread his wings and arched his back. He danced up on his toes. The feathers on his neck ruffled. He flapped his wings. He charged!

Yip! Yip! The poodles ran down the sidewalk like black and white streaks. The rooster chased them, darting and pecking. *Squawk! Squawk!*

"Emmy! You left the gate open again!" yelled Daniel, running after Peepers.

"Not me!" said Emmy. "It's Kelsey's fault!"

Peepers chased the poodles back into their own yard. But he didn't stop there. He circled the dogs, flapping his wings. Dot whined. Dash growled.

"My poor babies!" wailed Miss Clay. "Get that wild animal away!" She grabbed her broom. Kelsey screamed.

"No!" yelled Daniel. He splashed across the wet lawn, slipping a little in the mud. "Don't hurt him! He's just protecting the hens! I'll get him!"

He dived at Peepers and caught him. He settled the still angry rooster under his arm and carried him home.

Dad stood on the front steps. "What's going on?" he asked. "I heard noise." His eyes widened when he saw Peepers. "She's a rooster!" he exclaimed. Then he looked at Daniel. "Son," he said. "We need to talk."

Miss Clay had called the police to complain. After the police left, Dad had a long talk with the Secret Chicken Society. Even Tyler.

"It was wrong of you to try to keep Peepers a secret," Dad told them.

"We're sorry," said Daniel. "Are we grounded?"

"I think this is punishment enough," said Dad. He put his hand on Daniel's shoulder. "The police

have given us just fourteen days to find another home for Peepers."

Daniel tried to talk his parents into letting him keep the banty rooster. But it was no use.

"We can't break the law," said Dad. Daniel thought he looked a little bit sad.

"Besides," said Mom kindly, "this isn't the best place for a rooster. He needs a new home."

Daniel put posters up around town:

```
FREE TO GOOD HOME

NICE ROOSTER

WILL KEEP YOUR GARDEN FREE

OF SLUGS AND SNAILS
```

He called friends and relatives. He advertised in the newspaper. He even called Mrs. Lopez. Maybe she'd like to have Peepers for her classroom in the fall. But no one wanted a rooster.

All too soon the fourteen days were up. The whole family watched as the two officers pulled up in the police car. The tall one got out, carrying a wire cage.

For Peepers, thought Daniel. *Jailbird*. His throat tightened.

He felt Dad's hand on his shoulder. "Do you want to get him? Or do you want me to?" he asked.

"I'll do it," said Daniel.

Emmy held Mom's hand. She was crying. Kelsey's face was red. She cried, too. Even Tyler had nothing snarky to say.

The whole family and the policemen followed Daniel out back to the chicken coop.

Peepers scratched the dirt, looking for bugs. He cocked one eye at Daniel, and went back to scratching. He clearly had no idea what was coming.

Daniel sat down next to him in the dirt. He stroked his golden brown feathers. "I'll miss you," he said. Tears pricked his eyes. His vision blurred behind his glasses. He blinked. And saw Poison, a few feet away. Hiding in the bushes. Twitching his tail. Daniel's pent-up feelings burst loose.

"STUPID CAT!" he yelled, jumping up and waving his arms. "GET OUT OF HERE!"

Poison hissed. He sped under the fence. Daniel turned back to Peepers. "Well, this ought to make Mr. Gruffalo happy, anyhow," he grumbled. He picked up his rooster. He wished Mrs. Grafalo could say good-bye. At least she liked roosters.

"Wait a minute!" he yelled. He turned to the policemen. "Can I make one phone call?"

They looked at each other. "Please?" Daniel pleaded. "Even the bad guys on TV get one phone call." The stout officer shrugged.

Daniel put Peepers back into the chicken run. He grabbed Mom's hand and pulled her into the house.

Chapter 12

THE CHICKEN DANCE

That afternoon the whole family went to Willow-dale Care Center. Soft music still played. It still smelled like boiled cabbage and cleaning stuff.

Mom and Dad brought blackberries from the garden. Emmy brought more wildflowers. Kelsey brought banana bread. Tyler just brought himself.

Mr. Grafalo was there, too. He stood behind Mrs. G.'s wheelchair. He'd brought a cake for Mrs. G.'s birthday. He looked surprised to see Daniel carrying Peepers. He started to frown, but Mrs. G. held out her arms. Daniel handed Peepers to her. She cuddled the rooster. He fluffed his feathers. He sat in her lap just like a little dog.

"You brought the rooster!" said Mrs. G. She stroked his feathers.

"I talked to Ms. Benton this morning," Daniel told her. "She said Peepers can live here now. She said it would be good for all of the people at Willowdale to have a pet rooster to care for and love."

Mrs. G. set Peepers on the floor. The other residents came over to see. Peepers strutted around like he owned the place. He puffed out his chest. He fluffed his feathers. He did his funny little shuffle.

"He's doing the chicken dance!" said Mrs. G. Her eyes crinkled with laughter.

Peepers pranced over to Mr. Grafalo. He tugged on Mr. G.'s shoelace, and everyone laughed.

"He thinks it's a worm!" laughed Mrs. G. "Thank you for bringing him!" she said to Daniel.

"You get to keep Peepers here," said Daniel. He looked warily at Mr. Grafalo. What would he say? Would he say roosters belong in stew pots? But Mr. Grafalo wasn't looking at Daniel. He was watching Mrs. G.

And smiling.

DANIEL'S EGG JOURNAL

Do you know which came first—the chicken or the egg?
Neither do I, but in Mrs. Lopez's class, the eggs came first.
Here's how to hatch eggs:

Incubator. You need eggs and you need an incubator. Mrs.
Lopez strongly recommends buying one that turns the eggs auto-
matically. Then you don't have to go to school on the weekends
and do it. If you don't get an incubator with an automatic turner,
mark an X on one side of the egg and an O on the other so you can
turn them properly. You must turn the eggs side to side, not end to
end. Keep the small end pointed the same way every time. Do not
turn the eggs after day eighteen. Set up the incubator one week
before the eggs arrive. Follow the incubator instructions to set the
temperature and humidity.

Eggs. You can't hatch eggs from the grocery store, because they
aren't fertile. You must buy fertile eggs from a science supply
company like Carolina Biological Supply (www.carolina.com) or
a local farm store. You can choose eggs of all one breed of chicken
or mixed breeds like we did. Be careful with the eggs when they
arrive. Eggs with cracked shells will not hatch.

Put the eggs in the incubator as soon as they come. It takes
twenty-one days for chicken eggs to hatch. Check the temperature
and humidity twice a day and record them in your egg journal.

Candling. After eight to twelve days of incubation, you can
"candle" the eggs to see the embryo. Hold the egg up to a flashlight

or projector light. At first it just looks like a dark spot, but later you will see the heart beat. Cool!

<u>Hatching</u>. The eggs will start to hatch in twenty-one days.

You will hear a little tapping noise and see the egg rocking back and forth. Then the beak pokes out. This is called pipping. Lower the incubator temperature to 95 degrees. Lift the lid occasionally to let moisture out so the chicks can dry.

Brooder. A brooder is a structure for keeping chicks safe and warm. You can buy one, or make one out of a cardboard box. Move chicks to the brooder as soon as they are dry. The brooder should have a heat lamp. Cover the floor with straw or moss. The chicks don't need any food or water for a while, and then you can put in food trays and a water dish.

Giving the chicks a good home. Plan for where the chicks will live after the three weeks are up. They must not ever be released into the wild. A good home provides shelter, food, water, fresh air, exercise, and protection from predators. Never neglect, abuse, or abandon any animal.

Vocabulary Words You Need to Know:

Albumen—the white part inside the egg

Embryo—the unborn chick

Membrane—the thin covering inside the eggshell

Pipping—when the chick's beak pokes through the shell

Yolk—the yellow part inside the egg